SEESAW GIRL

YEARLING BOOKS are designed especially to entertain and enlighten young people. Patricia Reilly Giff, consultant to this series, received her bachelor's degree from Marymount College and a master's degree in history from St. John's University. She holds a Professional Diploma in Reading and a Doctorate of Humane Letters from Hofstra University. She was a teacher and reading consultant for many years, and is the author of numerous books for young readers.

SEESAW GIRL

BY **LINDA SUE PARK**

ILLUSTRATED BY JEAN AND MOU-SIEN TSENG

A YEARLING BOOK

To my parents:
My mother, who taught me to read
My father, who took me to the library

Published by
Dell Yearling
an imprint of
Random House Children's Books
a division of Random House, Inc.
1540 Broadway
New York, New York 10036

Visit us on the Web! www.randomhouse.com/kids

Educators and librarians, for a variety of teaching tools, visit us at
www.randomhouse.com/teachers

ISBN: 0-440-41672-8
Reprinted by arrangement with Houghton Mifflin Company
Printed in the United States of America
February 2001

10 9 8 7 6 5 4 3

OPM

Contents

SEESAW GIRL

Brushes and Ashes

"Is anyone coming?" Jade Blossom whispered.

Graceful Willow peeped around the edge of the sliding paper door. She looked back at Jade and shook her head, putting her finger to her lips.

Jade felt her insides trembling as she stole quietly to the opposite side of the room. Two dozen rabbit-hair writing brushes lay on the tidy shelf in an orderly row. The brushes were arranged by size, the smallest with the merest wisp of tip, the largest as wide as two fingers.

Jade snatched them up as quietly as she could. She hurried back across the room to where Willow stood guard by the door.

"Hurry!" begged Willow, handing her the bowl of ashes. "They might come back at any moment."

Jade unrolled a pile of old rags. She emptied the bowl of ashes and soot onto the rags and piled the brushes on top. Then she wrapped the rags carefully around the brushes. Rolling the untidy parcel around and around in her hands, she made sure that inside, every brush was well covered in soot.

Jade tiptoed back to the shelves, opened the parcel, and gingerly put the brushes back in their places. She stepped back, eyeing them for a moment. Both the handles and brush tips were black to begin with; the black of the soot could not be seen. Jade grinned, pleased with her work. This would surely be one of their best pranks ever.

From her lookout post, Willow gasped. "They're coming!" She turned back to Jade, beckoning wildly.

Jade darted to her side, and together they almost fell over the one-step threshold of the room. Hand in hand, breathless and laughing, they ran across the Inner Court to the safety of the women's quarters just as the boys came into view.

Schoolmaster had taken Jade's brothers and cousins to the Garden of Earthly Peace that afternoon. It was a beautiful spring day, and the plum trees were in bloom. The eight boys were then going to write poetry about what they had seen. Jade and Willow had been waiting for this opportunity to steal into the Hall of Learning while the boys were away.

Willow was Jade's aunt, but having fifteen years to Jade's twelve, she had always been more like a friend than an elder. Though it was Jade who planned their pranks, Willow was always on hand to lend support. This prank had taken several days of planning.

The boys would fetch the brushes and pots of ink from the shelves and begin to write on scrolls of fine rice paper. Their hands would be covered with soot, and they would blotch and smear their work. They would not be able to form the graceful characters demonstrated by Schoolmaster.

Jade and Willow knew well that none of the boys would utter a word of surprise or dismay. It was considered extremely rude to interrupt Schoolmaster's lessons. Rather, they would have to struggle along as best they could—and when their work was inspected . . . The girls could hardly wait for the reaction.

Hastily, they wiped out the bowl, discarded the rags, and washed their hands. Then they gathered up their embroidery projects and joined the other women and girls of the household in the women's hall.

Each worked on her own project, the older women talking quietly, the girls chatting more brightly. Sometimes one of the women would offer guidance to a daughter or niece, while the girls admired the work of their elders. It was a serene yet social time, a time Jade usually enjoyed.

But today she did not feel very serene; her laughter bubbled inside her like a rice pot ready to boil over. She fidgeted, unable to concentrate on her work, and had to pick out many of her stitches. Jade did not dare look at Willow for fear they would begin laughing again.

After a little while a loud voice could be heard from across the Inner Court. The women and girls raised their heads from their work and listened for a moment. Jade's mother shook her head, saying, "Schoolmaster is not pleased with the boys' work today. Tiger Heart and the others must work harder on their studies."

Willow let out an odd sound, like a snort, and quickly brought her hand to her mouth, as if to hide a cough. Jade felt as though she were strangling. She bent her head farther over her work and felt her stomach shaking with smothered laughter.

The rest of the afternoon passed pleasantly enough. At last Jade's mother folded her work, which was the signal for the other women and girls to put their work away as well. The gong sounded; dinner preparations would begin.

Just then the boys could be heard, calling out and running across the Inner Court. The whole group of them clamored around the door to the women's hall. They could not, of course, enter without permission from Jade's mother.

Jade's mother slid the paper door open. "What is it, Tiger Heart?" she asked, addressing Jade's older brother.

"Someone did something to the writing brushes!" he exclaimed breathlessly. "Our hands got all black—we couldn't write—" The other boys joined in, speaking all at

once indignantly and holding up their hands for everyone to see.

Eldest Aunt began to scold the boys. They had been in the garden, hadn't they? They had probably gotten their hands dirty fooling around, rather than paying attention to Schoolmaster. Besides, what did they expect to find in the women's hall? The girls had been busy all afternoon!

"Now, be on your way," said Eldest Aunt. "We have the evening meal to prepare." The women shooed the boys away from the door and left the room, with the girls following. Jade and Willow hung back and, when everyone else was out of earshot, finally gave in to their laughter. They shrieked until tears rolled down their cheeks. It was a good thing no one saw them. They too would have been scolded; such laughter was not proper for women or girls.

Laundry Sticks

The next day, however, the laundry was no laughing matter. The boys' soot-soiled clothing all had to be laundered, and it was far too much work for the maidservants alone. Jade and Willow were ordered to help.

The maidservants usually laundered most of the clothes for the household, but the Han women and girls did the important ceremonial clothes, and Jade's mother herself took care of her husband's clothing. His outfits were considered too important to be entrusted to the servants or younger women.

First, all the soiled clothes were ripped apart along the seams and hems. Everyone knew that flat pieces of cloth could be more thoroughly cleaned and smoothly pressed than the garments themselves. Once the clothes had been ripped apart, they were washed and hung to dry.

Then the dried clothes were beaten to get rid of all the wrinkles. Jade hated this part most of all. The flat pieces of cloth were laid on a flat stone and beaten with two round wooden sticks. Jade had to pound at the clothes until her arms ached and her hands were sore. The tattoo beat of laundry sticks sounded constantly in the Han house, sometimes even into the night. Finally, the clothes were sewn back together again.

Wearing clean clothes daily was a luxury only the wealthy could afford. Jade's mother and aunts saw to it that the members of the Han family were always clothed in a manner worthy of their place in society. There were times like today, as she bent for hours over the sticks, when Jade thought a lower place in society and a little less laundry would not be such a bad thing.

———————————

Jade and Willow were rarely punished for their pranks. Jade's mother might scold them when their mischief was discovered, but she also forbade any retaliation by the boys. They tried nonetheless; Tiger Heart had once succeeded in dropping several small green caterpillars down the necks of the girls' short linen jackets. But Jade had noticed that Tiger had lost interest in retaliating lately, and to her relief, none of the younger boys had stepped into his place.

Jade had also heard her mother speak calming words to Eldest Aunt when the girls' mischief was discovered.

"It's not proper behavior for girls," Aunt had protested.

"No harm has been done," Jade's mother replied.

On hearing this, Jade kept her head bowed so that Eldest Aunt would not see the look of satisfaction she could not keep from her face.

One warm afternoon in early summer Jade thought the pounding of laundry would drive her crazy. She paused to rest her aching forearms for a moment. Beside her, Willow was sewing the pressed pieces of cloth into garments again. She had worked her way through a pile of such pieces, putting the finished clothes into a basket at her side.

Willow had just completed one of Tiger Heart's jackets. As she put it aside and reached for the pieces of the trousers, Jade seized her arm.

"Wait, Willow! I have an idea . . ."

The two girls bent their heads together.

Jade whispered excitedly, "You could sew a seam across the bottoms of the legs. And when Tiger tries to put them on, his feet will get stuck!"

Willow giggled, automatically putting her hand in front of her mouth. It was considered impolite for a woman to show her teeth when smiling or laughing. Then she shook her head at Jade.

"That *would* be funny. But I don't want to do it. The trousers might get torn. Then we'd really get into trouble."

"Please! I can't do it myself. The others might notice—you know I'm not allowed to sew clothes back together yet. Eldest Aunt doesn't think my stitching is good enough."

The smile faded from Willow's face, and she shook her head again more firmly.

"No. Let's just go to the garden after we're finished here. It's a beautiful day . . ."

Jade slumped back in disappointment. Willow had never before refused to go along with one of her pranks.

"You go to the garden. I have other things to do."

Willow looked stricken for a moment, then pressed her lips together and dropped her eyes to her work. Jade felt a twinge of regret. She hadn't meant to quarrel. But it was such a good idea! Why was Willow being so stubborn?

Jade went back to thumping sullenly at the laundry.

The girls finished their work in silence. Willow knotted the thread for the last seam, folded the trousers, and laid them on top of the neat pile in the basket. Then she stood and walked toward the door.

Jade hesitated only a moment. "Wait, Willow! I'll go with you." Willow's face lit with a smile, and the two girls skipped to the garden together. Jade's heart felt as light as her steps; she couldn't imagine even a single afternoon without her dearest friend.

Within the Walls

Jade Blossom lived in a beautiful house in the middle of Seoul. Her family was highly respected because her father was an important adviser to the king.

Jade's family was not just her mother and father and two brothers. Along with Willow, three uncles and their wives and children—twelve cousins in all—lived in the house too.

But it was big enough for all of them—and for the gate-keeper, the cook, the stableboys, the maidservants, the gardener, and Schoolmaster. The Han house was one of the finest in all of Seoul.

The house was built like a **U** around the Inner Court.

The women lived in one part. The men's rooms were at the front, near the gate to the Outer Court. There was the Great Hall for family gatherings and ceremonial days, and the Hall of Learning for the boys' lessons. The Garden of Earthly Peace was at the back of the Inner Court.

The Outer Court was surrounded by a wall. Inside the wall were the servants' rooms and the stables.

Yes, it was a fine house—and it was Jade Blossom's whole world.

It was the custom for women and girls in noble families to be protected from strange men. As a little girl Jade had been allowed to play in the Outer Court, feeding grain to the horses or helping the servants gather eggs. When she reached the age of eight, however, even the Outer Court was forbidden.

Since then Jade had not been allowed to set foot outside the Inner Court. Her mother, aunts, and girl cousins—none of them ever went beyond the Inner Court except on the rare occasion of a wedding. Jade would be allowed to leave her home only twice in the future—to attend Tiger Heart's wedding at the home of the bride, and finally to move to the home of her husband after her own wedding.

Jade and all her girl cousins knew that this was the way of things. None of her cousins minded too much. There was always plenty to do in the Inner Court. Jade was learning to embroider. She hoped one day to be as skilled as her mother. Her mother could paint with a needle and thread—a fierce red dragon snorting fire, a willow tree that seemed to move in the wind. She had made a beautiful silk pouch for Jade, padded and lined with more silk. In it Jade kept her most treasured possession—a carved ivory ball.

Jade had once seen a flock of cranes fly over the garden. That picture was in her head now, and someday, when she had skill enough, she would make it come alive with a million tiny stitches. For now, she practiced embroidering flowers on scraps of silk.

When the sewing, embroidering, and laundry were done for the day, there was time to play. Jade and Willow loved the Garden of Earthly Peace. It was quiet there, in a far corner of the Court away from the beat of the laundry sticks. Willow trees and irises surrounded a little pond. A bridge arched gracefully over the pond.

The two girls would stand on the bridge and watch the fish swim. It was usually on the bridge that their little pranks were discussed, out of earshot of the rest of the household.

There were frogs in the garden. Jade and Willow caught them sometimes, and put them in a box to watch them jump. Once they had even put one in a rice bowl—then waited just outside the kitchen to hear the cook's outraged screech. But they always let the frogs go afterward.

Jade would often bring her precious ivory ball to the garden. She and Willow would take turns hiding it for the other to find.

It was a miniature version of a much larger and more intricate ball in her father's room. That one was the size of a full-blown peony bloom. It was hollow and held another, smaller ball. The second ball held another ball, and so on, and so on, forever. Or so Jade had thought as a child. Tiger Heart had once told her that there were actually only a dozen balls, but Jade preferred to think that the balls decreased in size until they were too small to see.

Her greatest wonder over this marvel was reserved for the nameless person who had made it. How had he sculpted its lovely flowers, leaves, and birds? There were no seams on any of the balls; it had been carved from a solid piece of ivory. Jade could not even imagine how the artist had accomplished such a trick. How long had it taken him? What had been in his mind as he planned and created such a lovely thing?

The King had presented Jade's father with the ball as a mark of favor many years before. It had been a gift from the Chinese court. As a small child, Jade had crept into her father's room on many occasions to stare at it.

At last year's New Year celebration, to her great surprise and delight, her father had given her the tiny carved ball. Only then had Jade realized that her father knew of her interest in the large one. The little ball immediately became her good-luck charm, and although she knew it was unlikely, she liked to think that the same person had made both balls. Whenever it was her turn to be the seeker of the ball, Jade felt that she was hunting treasure.

It was during such a game of hide-and-find, a few days after refusing to go along with the pants prank, that Willow told Jade the news.

A Goose for the Wedding

There was tremendous excitement in the Han household on this midsummer day. Graceful Willow was getting married.

The matchmaker had visited a few months earlier with word that a man of good family sought Willow for his bride. As Jade's paternal grandparents had both gone to the Heavenly Kingdom, it was her father, Willow's eldest brother, who stood in for them and agreed to the match.

Everyone was scurrying about making last-minute preparations. Jade Blossom sat in the women's quarters watching Willow get ready for the ceremony.

Watching when she could, that is. Jade's mother and El-dest Aunt kept calling out orders: "Get some more hair oil! Where is the comb? Fetch a needle and thread! Hurry!"

They were not the only ones who were busy. The other aunts were in the kitchen, supervising the final touches on the lavish wedding banquet. The servants flew about with a hundred tasks. And Jade's father, as head of the household, was inspecting the Great Hall, where the ceremony would take place.

Willow was ready. Her long red silk skirt flowed out from under a bright green jacket. Around her waist she wore a belt with heavily embroidered tassels. Her hair was twisted into an elaborate bun that had been lacquered until it gleamed like a mirror. An intricate wedding headdress rested atop her head. Her face had been powdered until it was as white as paper, her kohl-drawn eyebrows arched delicately, and her lips were stained ruby red.

Jade couldn't stop staring at Willow. For as long as she could remember, Willow had been beside her as they worked on their household tasks. After the work was done, they had spent many happy afternoons together in the gar-den. Jade could not recall ever having been without Wil-low's cheerful companionship.

Now she looked like a stranger. She looked so grown-up, so beautiful, that Jade was almost afraid to speak to her. But as they left the women's quarters to go across the Inner Court to the Great Hall where the ceremony would take place, Jade stepped forward and handed Willow a small package.

"What's this?" Willow asked with a smile. She opened the rice-paper wrapping carefully. Inside was a small purse in the traditional shape—a drawstring pouch made of silk and brightly embroidered. Jade had made it herself.

"It's lovely." Following tradition, Jade had covered the front of the purse with bright flowers. On the back such a purse would have a single Chinese character indicating perhaps "luck" or "happiness." Chinese characters were considered more poetic than their Korean equivalents. Willow turned the purse over.

Instead of a Chinese word, Jade had embroidered a rabbit-hair brush. Willow looked up quickly; their eyes met and danced together briefly.

But Eldest Aunt was impatient, as always. "Come, Willow! It's time!"

The Great Hall had been specially prepared for the ceremony. There were finely woven straw mats and silk cushions covering the floor on either side of the room, with a long, low table in the center. Jade's father led the family into the Hall and took his place on one side of the room, with his three brothers at his side. All their sons sat behind them. Jade sat with the women and girls, clustered in one corner of the room; Willow took her place at the central table.

Jade's father rose from his place when the gatekeeper an-

nounced the arrival of the groom's family. As the great door to the Hall opened wide to admit the guests, Jade could see part of the long line of sedan chairs that had carried the women and girls.

They arrived at dusk, the traditional time for a lucky wedding. Candles burned to light the Great Hall. The groom's parents entered first and exchanged deep bows with Jade's father. They were followed by the groom himself, then the other members of his family—twenty in all.

Jade watched eagerly for the groom's entrance. He came into the room carrying a wild goose under one arm. He placed the goose on the central table and took his place opposite Willow.

Jade had attended the weddings of all three of her uncles. She had been too young to remember anything about the first two. But the wedding of her third uncle a few years ago had been one of the most exciting days of her young life. With her mother she had been carried in a sedan chair to the house of the bride's parents. There had been a wonderful feast, and other children to meet and play with. Of all Jade's memories of that day, it was the goose she remembered most clearly.

It was known that a pair of geese mated for life, so the groom always brought a wild goose to the wedding as the symbol of perfect faithfulness. The goose was placed on the table and remained there throughout the ceremony.

Then it was taken outside and released, whereupon it presumably found its mate again.

At the wedding of Jade's uncle the goose had refused to stay on the table. It had run about the room, squawking and flapping in a most undignified manner. Jade and the other children had jumped to their feet, laughing and pointing, and she had never forgotten the severe reprimand she had received from her mother on her behavior at such a solemn occasion. The problem had been solved by releasing the goose a little sooner than was usual.

Now Jade watched closely so as not to miss any excitement. When the groom placed the goose on the table, he stroked its feathers gently and put a small handful of grain before it. The goose settled down and pecked calmly at the grain. Jade had not wanted Willow's wedding ceremony to be spoiled by an ill-mannered goose, but even so, she was a little disappointed that this goose behaved so well.

Later, Tiger Heart told her that the groom had caught the goose several days before the wedding and kept it about the house, training it to keep still with handfuls of grain. Jade thought it was a good omen for Willow that her new husband showed such foresight.

When the groom's family was all assembled on the other side of the room, the ceremony began. First there was the bowing. The groom bowed once to Jade's father, Willow bowed twice to the groom's parents. Then the sequence was repeated. These were the traditional bows of deepest respect; each bow took a full minute or more to complete. The groom bent his knees slowly until they touched the ground, then lowered his forehead to the ground. Willow finished her bows in a seated pose, with her forehead likewise on the ground. She was required to bow twice as many times as the groom to signify the weaker position of the woman.

Then the bride and groom faced each other across the low table. They shared three spoonfuls of rice and drank rice wine from special marriage bowls. The two bowls had been carved from a single gourd, to show how the two people were parts of the same soul now.

Finally the couple stood and bowed together, first to the groom's parents and then to Jade's father. The groom picked up the goose and strode to the door of the hall. Everyone watched as he opened the door and threw the goose into the air.

That was the signal for merriment. The servants began to bring in tray after tray of food and rice wine, and the celebration began in earnest. Jade jumped to her feet to help her mother and aunts serve the men. Amid the sudden burst of activity she saw Willow, still seated at the central table.

For the entire ceremony and the party that followed, Willow was forbidden to eat or drink anything except the ceremonial rice and wine. She was also forbidden to smile or speak to anyone. Her complete silence and sobriety would demonstrate the depth of her virtue to her new family.

Jade had forgotten this part until now. Seeing Willow alone and motionless in the middle of the room, while all around her people ate and drank and laughed, Jade felt a lump rise in her throat. She could not cry, for she knew that tears at a wedding might bring the couple terrible luck.

Jade realized then what she had been trying not to think about ever since she had first heard about the wedding. This might be the last time she ever saw Willow. Now that she was married, Willow would never again return to the house of Han. She belonged to their family no more.

Thread with No End

After Willow's departure, not a single hour went by in which Jade did not think of her. Jade played with her other cousins once in a while, but all of them were younger and none felt like a real friend. Without Willow, Jade did not even have the heart to plan pranks anymore.

Jade was now the oldest girl in the house. She had to do more of the household work and had less time to play. She was learning to sew the garments back together after they had been pounded smooth; before, she had been trusted only to rip them apart. Jade's mother and aunts scolded her about her sewing: Her seams were not straight enough; she sewed too slowly.

Jade realized that these new responsibilities had been Willow's before. Willow had never complained. She had done her work cheerfully and well, and always had time to spend with Jade. But Jade hated sewing as she had always hated pounding the laundry. She liked embroidery, for she liked seeing how the colored stitches slowly joined to make a picture. But sewing clothes together only to have them ripped apart again?

One day, when she had pricked her finger for what seemed like the hundredth time, she asked Eldest Aunt, "Why can't we just wash the clothes as they are? Why do we have to rip them apart and sew them back together all the time?"

Her aunt, harried and busy, answered impatiently. "Silly girl! Don't you know that dirt hides in the stitching, in all the pockets and corners? Wherever there is dirt, the spirits of sickness can hide too! Ripping the clothes apart is the only way to get them truly clean. Now stop asking such stupid questions. No man will want a wife who thinks in such a lazy way."

Jade bent over her sewing once again. The thread twisted and made yet another terrible knot that she had to unpick little by little. As she threaded the needle again, she thought of all the stitches she would have to sew in her lifetime, and the thread seemed to have no end.

Jade's brother Tiger Heart was the oldest son of the oldest son of the house of Han. As such he had many responsibilities, but also many privileges. It was he who accompanied their father on his trips up the mountain on all the important feast days. There they visited the family shrine and honored their dead ancestors with gifts and prayers.

"Elder Brother, what is it like there?" Jade asked him when he returned from one such journey.

Tiger thought for a moment. He tried to explain. "The mountains look so far away when you first start on the road. They get closer and closer, but even when you reach the lower hills, the top still looks far away.

"Our ancestors' gravesite is not quite halfway up. When you get there, you can turn and look back down the mountain. Then you can see the line of people, like a snake, going far down the road, all of them going to their ancestors' graves."

Jade asked more questions. Tiger told her about the worship ceremony, when he and their father laid gifts of food and small amounts of money on the stone altar. He told her how they tidied the gravesite, clearing weeds and planting shrubs and flowers. He talked about the grand picnic they had on the way back down, in a little clearing cooled by a bubbling stream.

Jade listened with all her heart. She tried to make pictures in her head of what Tiger told her. One day she discovered that if she stood in a certain spot in the center of the garden, she could just make out the mountain peaks beyond the Outer Court walls. After that she would stand in the spot every day and look; on some days the peaks were hidden by thick clouds, and even on clear days the very tops were all she could see.

It was almost worse than not being able to see the mountains at all. How hard it was to imagine things that she had never seen!

———————

Tiger also went out with the servants on market days. He always had a few *won* in his pocket to throw at a passing juggler or to buy sweets. Tiger was a good brother. He always brought home sweets for Jade and their younger brother, Mountain Wind.

But Jade wanted more than sweets. Whenever Tiger returned from one of his forays to the market, she plied him with questions.

"What was the market like today? Was it very crowded? Was the magician there?"

"No, Jade," said Tiger. "The magician was not there today. But there was a traveling jester. He was even better than the magician. He could juggle three rings while running about the main square and singing a funny song at the same time!"

Jade tried to imagine such a sight. She fetched three carved wooden bracelets from her room and gave them to Tiger. He began running around the Inner Court, pretending to juggle and singing at the top of his lungs. Jade and the cousins laughed at him.

Encouraged by their laughter, Jade got up to try. She took the bracelets from Tiger and tried running backward, tossing them up and catching them all the while. Everyone was laughing when she crashed right into Eldest Aunt, who was carrying a fresh jar of *kimchee*.

"*Ai-go!*" shouted Eldest Aunt. The jar of pickled cabbage was jostled from her hands, but she caught it just in time. "Jade Blossom! You are too old for such foolishness. What are you doing here anyway? I heard your mother calling you. She needs help with the evening meal. Go!"

The laughter died away. Jade soberly straightened her clothes and hair and went to find her mother. For the thousandth time Jade wondered what Willow was doing now.

Baskets to Market

More than two months had passed since Willow's wedding, and Jade could stand it no longer. She knew that neither of them was allowed to leave her home, but she had to see Willow again, no matter what. Jade needed a plan.

Over the next month she watched the servants carefully. She saw that every few days they went to the kitchens and emptied the last of the vegetables from the huge baskets in which they were stored. The baskets were taken to the Outer Court. Later that morning they were returned, full of fresh vegetables.

So Jade knew that the baskets had been taken to the

market. The next time Tiger returned from market day, she asked him how it was done.

"They load the baskets onto a cart, and one of the oxen pulls it. Why do you want to know?" he asked.

"Oh, no reason," Jade replied. But the plan was beginning to form.

Jade knew that the baskets were big enough for her to squat down in so she could not be seen. But she did not know how she would get to the Outer Court and into a basket without anyone seeing her. There would be servants everywhere.

Jade was patient. She planned carefully. A few days later she watched as the baskets were taken out of the kitchen. Jade then began counting on her fingers to find out how long it took for the cart to be loaded. For every ten counts, she made a mark on the ground with a stick. She had made eleven marks when she heard the Outer Gate open and the steady clop of the ox's hoofs as the cart was driven away. Jade decided that there would be enough time for her to get into a basket—if she could distract the servants somehow.

The day before her planned escape, Jade saved scraps from all her meals. By the end of the day she had a piece of linen cloth filled with chicken bones, bits of meat, and balls of rice. She tied the corners of the cloth together and buried the parcel in the garden.

Jade rose the next morning to a perfect fall day. The sun

was warm, a crisp breeze blew, and the sky was the clear blue of the finest porcelain. An omen, Jade thought, a sign that today was the day. When she dressed, she added one item to her usual attire: She took the carved ivory ball from its silk bag and put it into her pocket.

Jade could hardly swallow her breakfast that morning. Fortunately, her mother did not notice how much food she left uneaten. Jade dutifully helped clean up after the morning meal, feeling her stomach grow tight with excitement. She finished her chores in time to see the servants carry the baskets to the Outer Court.

Jade took a deep breath. She ran to the garden, pulled out the parcel of food scraps, and ran back to the Inner Court. She was almost out of time.

She untied the corners of the cloth almost all the way. With all her might, she flung the parcel over the Inner Court wall.

It landed, as she had planned, near the hens' nests, which were lined up in a neat row under their little roof against the Outer Court wall. The household dogs, who prowled about the Outer Court, smelled it at once. They bounded eagerly past the stables and grappled with one another to try to reach the tasty scraps.

Meanwhile, of course, the hens were in a terrible frenzy. The squawking and barking brought all the servants running—including those who had been busy loading the cart.

Jade peered about the Inner Court. She could hear the laundry sticks and Schoolmaster's voice. No one was watching.

Clutching the little ivory ball for luck, Jade dashed through the gatekeeper's door. Everything was going perfectly. There were no servants nearby—and there in front of her, just before the Outer Gate, was the cart!

Jade's heart was beating so hard that she felt sure her mother would hear it. She pulled up her long skirts awkwardly and clambered onto the cart. She took the cover off the nearest basket. There were some old cabbage leaves at the bottom. They didn't smell very good, but Jade had no more time. She climbed into the basket, crouched down, and pulled the lid back on.

The squawking and barking subsided, and she heard footsteps returning to the cart. The servant climbed onto the front seat and tapped the ox with a stick. Off they went—ox, servant, and stowaway.

The Road to Willow

Crouched and uncomfortable in her hiding place, Jade was nonetheless elated. Her plan had worked! Now all she had to do was get out of the basket at the marketplace and figure out where the house of Lee was. That was Willow's home now.

Jade had questioned Tiger extensively about the marketing routine. He had answered her questions as he always did, annoyance balanced by good humor. From his description she knew that the servant would leave the ox grazing under a tree, then enter the marketplace to do the buying. After a time he would return to the cart and fill the baskets with his purchases.

Jade felt the cart bumping over the road for what seemed like hours. When the cart stopped, Jade waited still longer, to be sure that the servant had left to do the marketing. She had a bit of luck: The servant greeted a friend as he was tending to the ox, and she could hear their voices fade away. She peeped out of the basket.

She saw a crowd of people, most of them poorly dressed and carrying heavy loads on their *jiggehs*, the homemade wooden frames that served as backpacks. This was exciting enough for Jade, who rarely saw people from outside her own family. But an even greater surprise awaited her.

She saw *girls*. Women and girls! There were girls in the crowd—girls her age, with their mothers and grandmothers. Jade could not believe her eyes. Who were these girls, and why did their families allow them to leave their Inner Courts?

When Jade had recovered from her amazement, her mind returned to the task at hand. She waited for a moment when the passing crowd had thinned a little. No one noticed as she hopped out of the basket and climbed down from the cart. Cautiously she made her way to the road to join the crowds as they walked toward the marketplace.

There were so many people! Carts, oxen, chickens, and dogs added to the fray; dust rose in billowing clouds from the road. How would she ever find the house of Lee in this mess?

It was then that Jade discovered she had made a mistake. She had given no thought to any kind of disguise. She was wearing her everyday clothes. They were made of fine linen, and while they lacked the brilliant colors of her best silk dresses, they were still unmistakably the clothes of a girl from a noble family.

The crowd began to notice her. First a woman nudged her companions, and soon others were spreading the word that a wealthy girl was on the road. Jade realized what was happening as more and more eyes turned to her. She began to feel panic rising inside her when suddenly she felt a tug on her sleeve.

Jade looked down to see a child about seven years old next to her. The child was dressed in coarse rags, and Jade could not tell if it was a boy or a girl. But there was a look of lively curiosity on its face.

The child tugged again and addressed her respectfully. "Pardon me, mistress. Are you rich?"

Pleased by the child's politeness, Jade answered seriously. "I never thought about it. My father is an adviser to the King. Does that make me rich?"

"Oh, yes! And I've met lots of rich people. The men and boys come to the marketplace all the time. I've talked to the servants a lot too. But this is the first time I've ever talked to a rich *girl*."

The child's friendliness made Jade feel less lost, and it occurred to her that the child might be of some help. She spoke while moving off to the side of the road, where she hoped she would be less conspicuous. "Even if I am rich, I still need help."

"What kind of help, mistress?"

"I am looking for the house of Lee. Perhaps you know it. Mr. Lee also works at the court of the King."

The child frowned for a moment. "Would that be the Lee household that had such a grand wedding a few months ago?"

Jade felt hope and excitement wash over her. "Yes, yes, that's the one."

"It was great fun! We followed the wedding parade all the way to the house, and the servants threw sweets to us. I didn't get as many sweets as my brother—he's older than me—but still I got three, and that's more than I've ever had, even at New Year's—"

"Could you tell me where the house is?" Jade interrupted. "If you do, I'll try to get some more sweets for you. My brother comes to the market often. I'll ask him to give you some."

"My name is Chang. My family sells cabbages in the market. We usually have the third stall on the right."

"Yes, all right," Jade said impatiently. "Where is the house of Lee?"

The child pointed. "Follow the road past the marketplace. Just beyond, the road will fork. Take the left fork—if you went to the right, you would come to the King's palace! Have you ever been there? They say it has more than a hundred rooms! I've been to the gates often. Sometimes I stand there and try to see what's inside when they open the gates. But I can't stay long, because the guards usually chase us off—"

"I go to the left," Jade prompted her voluble instructor.

"That's right, and you walk a little ways and you'll come to a bridge over a stream. It will probably take you a little while to cross it, because everyone else will be coming the other way, it being the morning—"

Whether from the child's incessant prattling or from her own unfamiliarity with the place, Jade began to feel apprehensive. She interrupted again to say, "Why can't you show me the way yourself?"

The child's face dimmed momentarily. "Oh, I couldn't. I really shouldn't even be spending so much time talking to you now. I have to go back and help my family at the market. But don't worry, the house isn't hard to find. Once you're past the bridge, you keep walking—you'll be able to see the house already—it's the biggest house you can see from there."

Jade sighed inwardly; she would have liked the child's company. But she listened carefully and repeated the directions back to the child. Then she asked, "Would you help me with one more thing?"

The child was obliging and, following Jade's instructions, picked up handfuls of road dust and rubbed them all over her clothes. Jade furthered their efforts by stamping up more dust, even sitting down on the ground so the child could cover her thoroughly with dirt. Her companion giggled with delight at the unusual task and did not bother to ask for an explanation. When at last they finished and the dust had settled, Jade's clothes, while not ragged or coarse, fit in a great deal better with the crowd.

Just then, shouts could be heard from far down the road. Jade and her companion looked up. A cloud of dust rose in the distance, signaling that a great many people were hurrying toward them.

Prisoners

Word traveled faster than the crowd, and long before the commotion reached the marketplace, the people around them were buzzing with the news. Jade turned to her companion in puzzlement and was about to speak when the child suddenly dashed into the road. Chang spoke animatedly to a man for a few moments, then ran back to Jade.

"What is it? What's happening?"

"They're bringing the strangers! They're taking them to the palace!"

Not waiting for her reply, Chang whirled away again and joined many others who were rushing to meet the approaching throng.

Strangers? What was the child talking about? With the noise and chaos growing louder and more confusing every moment, Jade did not dare to step into the road again. She moved a few more steps in the direction the child had indicated would take her to the house of Lee, then half concealed herself behind a tree. The commotion had drawn most of the people from the marketplace; they were lining up on either side of the road. She did not want to be spotted by the servant.

Jade did not have long to wait. Soon the great crowd reached them—the first people running or trotting, most of them shouting angrily. They were followed by a phalanx of soldiers; she recognized their splendid scarlet uniforms and armor from having heard Tiger's descriptions of them.

The soldiers—hundreds of them, it seemed—marched impassively, forming a guard around several groups of men. Jade could not see their faces clearly at first, but she saw that there were more prisoners than she could count on her fingers. The prisoners were chained together and held roughly by soldiers who pushed them along. The din had grown to a roar by the time the soldiers drew level with her, so no one heard the cry of surprise that rose from Jade's throat. The prisoners looked like no men she had ever seen. They had red faces, with eyes that seemed to have no color at all and noses that protruded like the beaks of birds. Several had what seemed to be yellow or brown sheep's wool on their cheeks and chins; a few had hair—it must have been hair, for it covered the top of their heads—but how could it be hair? For it was the color of straw.

Chang had said they were being taken to the palace. Why? And why were the onlookers so angry? A thousand questions jostled in Jade's head until it felt as crowded and confused as the scene before her.

Most of the people along the road followed the soldiers and their prisoners. As the remaining crowd thinned, Jade caught a glimpse of Chang and hurried to catch up.

"What is it? Where are they going?" she panted, trotting alongside.

"They're taking them to the palace!" Chang shouted breathlessly. "They're going to chop their heads off!"

It took a moment for Jade to comprehend what the child had said. She almost tripped as she ran and made a desperate grab for Chang.

"Why? What have they done?" she asked, holding the child's arm.

"Don't you know? They're not allowed to be here— they've broken the law!" Chang shook off her hand impatiently and disappeared into the crowd.

The din was fading, and with it some of the noise in Jade's head seemed to quiet down too. She stood still, trying to piece together what Chang had told her. Those men were criminals. What had they done? What law had they broken? And where had they come from?

She recalled the faces of the strangers—the odd color of their skin, their pale eyes, and their beaked noses. Surely no good people looked like that.

The Gatekeeper

Jade had almost forgotten her original intention. Willow! Her husband worked in the court of the King—perhaps Willow would know the answers to her questions.

With the road quiet again, she remembered the child's directions and set out for the house of Lee. The old wooden bridge with its rickety railing was just wide enough for a man to pass with his ox or donkey alongside. Thanks to the excitement caused by the soldiers and their prisoners, the bridge was empty, and she crossed easily. As she walked to the gate of the Lee house, Jade felt a shiver of anticipation. She would soon be reunited with Willow again!

The door in the outer wall opened a crack as Jade approached. She could see the gatekeeper's eye peering through the opening. The gatekeeper barked rudely, "What do you want?"

Jade was indignant at being addressed in such a way by a servant. She drew herself up and made her voice as dignified as possible. "I am here to see Graceful Willow. Please tell her it is her niece."

The gatekeeper scolded her. "You are not her niece! How dare you come to this house in such falseness! Get away with you, pig girl!"

Jade's eyes blazed with anger. "I am her niece! Go and tell her that Jade Blossom is here. If you do not, I will see to it that you are severely punished."

The gatekeeper had been ready to slam the door shut, but as Jade watched, he hesitated and inspected her closely. Jade glanced down at her dirty clothes. She looked up again when the gatekeeper spoke.

"I will tell the mistress that you are here. But if you are not who you say you are . . ." He did not need to finish the threat. The punishment for such impudence, Jade knew, was a severe paddling. In her own household the heavy wooden paddles hung in the gatekeeper's quarters, ready to be used against impudent peddlers or beggars.

The door closed. Jade waited. It seemed a long time before it opened again.

The gatekeeper seemed triumphant. "The mistress says

that no girl from the house of Han would ever dare present herself as you have! She refuses to see you. Now be off with you!"

"No!" Jade cried out in horror. "I am her niece! Please—" She looked around wildly as if for help, then groped for the ivory ball in her pocket. "Take this to her. It will prove that I am who I say!"

The gatekeeper ignored her outstretched hand. "I will not bother the mistress again, you stupid girl! And I do not understand, but the mistress did not wish for you to be punished. She told me merely to send you away. Go!"

The door slammed. Jade staggered as if her face had been slapped. She knew it would be useless to try again.

As she trudged back toward the marketplace, Jade's numbed mind slowly recovered. The girl at the gate was not to be punished—those were Willow's orders. She must have suspected that it might indeed be Jade. Why had Willow refused to see her?

Jade did not want to think about it anymore. She arrived at the marketplace just in time to see the servant loading the baskets full of vegetables back onto the cart, and she realized dispiritedly that her failure to see Willow had left her without a plan for the return journey. She had assumed that Willow would order a sedan chair to take her home. And she could not go the way she had come, for the baskets were full now.

There was nothing else for it. Jade walked right up to the servant and asked him to take her home.

The servant's eyes nearly popped out of his head. "*Ai-go, ai-go,* young mistress—what will your mother say?" Greatly agitated, he ran back into the marketplace and returned with a length of new cloth. He helped Jade onto the seat of the cart and threw the cloth over her, somewhat belatedly hiding her from the eyes of strangers.

Jade was too discouraged to protest. But on the journey home she found she could arrange the cloth to keep most of her head and body covered while leaving a peephole for one eye. She saw the people on the road again, and other things she had not noticed in the earlier turmoil.

She saw the watery green fields of rice beyond the road. She saw a stork picking its way through the water, and cattle grazing at the roadside. And she saw, with awe and wonder, the blue-gray mountains in the far distance.

Jade caught her breath. The mountains towered over the city, yet the mists that shrouded them somehow gentled their power. The mountains seemed at once mysterious and familiar, and Jade marveled that ordinary things like rock and earth and trees could rise to such magnificence.

Somehow their great solidity was a comfort to her, smoothing out the roiled thoughts of all she had done and seen that morning. In spite of the confusion in her head, the mountains would never change. Somewhere on those misty gray slopes were the ancestral graves of her family, where Tiger and her father went with the other men on feast days. She wondered what it would be like to actually walk those slopes, and knew with a pain in her heart that she would do so only in her dreams.

Jade looked at the mountains as long as she could, until the cart turned into the Outer Court and her mother came running.

A Willing Heart

It did not take long for Jade to realize that her plan had failed in more ways than one. Her mother was so angry that she did not even speak at first. When Jade climbed down from the cart at the gate to the Inner Court, her mother merely gestured for her to go to the kitchens, as it was time for the noon meal.

Jade felt as though she had been gone for days, but the pattern of the household had continued unchanged in her absence. The men ate first, served by the women. Helping her mother and aunts wait on the men, Jade found that she could hardly even look at her father. Although he was always aloof and reserved with the children, she felt that his countenance was even more severe than usual. Later, when the women and girls ate, Jade sat silently, her face burning, while all the aunts and girl cousins whispered behind their hands and stared at her.

Jade and her brothers loved and respected their father, but as head of the Han household he did not have much idle time to spend with them. It was their mother who looked after such family matters as the disciplining of the children. After dinner that evening, Jade was summoned to her mother's room.

Her mother spoke quietly. "I think you already know that what you did today was very wrong, Jade. It was not just one thing. It was many things. You deceived your family. You went into the road, where strange men could see you. You could have gotten lost, or hurt. You have brought great shame to our household. You were very lucky that nothing worse happened."

Jade bowed very low, as was the custom. Hunched over on the ground, she felt much smaller and younger than her twelve years. She whispered, "I am sorry, Honorable Mother, that I brought shame to our family."

"What were you doing, Jade? Did you want sweets from the market? Tiger Heart can always bring you what you want."

Jade heard the gentleness in her mother's voice. She raised her head. "No, Mother. I went to the house of Lee. I wanted to see Graceful Willow again."

Her mother was silent for a moment. Then she asked, "Did you succeed?"

Jade bowed her head again. She whispered, "No, Mother. Willow would not see me."

"Do you know why?"

Jade shook her head.

"Jade, Willow is no longer your aunt. Now she is the wife of the oldest son of the house of Lee. That is a great responsibility. How would it look to the Lees if they were to learn that a member of our family could behave so dishonorably? Graceful Willow is a dutiful girl. She sent you home so as not to dishonor her new family."

Jade could not look at her mother. She did not want to believe these words, yet somehow she felt that they must be true.

Her mother was still speaking. "I have decided that as your punishment you will beat the family laundry for five days, by yourself. But not only with your hands—you must do it with a willing heart."

Jade nodded numbly. "Yes, Mother. It shall be so." She longed to speak to her mother of the things she had seen that morning, but it was not her place to do so unless her mother brought up the subject first.

Jade's mother looked at her daughter for a long moment. "Little Jade . . . Do not think that I do not understand. I know that life in the Inner Court sometimes lacks excitement. But I wish to tell you something that you will learn

for yourself when you are older." She walked to the paper door of the room and slid it open.

"Come stand here with me, Jade," she said. They stood together and looked out over the Inner Court. It was quiet now. Lanterns hung at the corners of the buildings, and the rooms beyond glowed golden behind their paper doors. Jade could hear voices and occasionally laughter.

"At the end of the day, when I am so tired from the laundry and preparing the food and caring for all the people in our household, sometimes I stand here like this. Everyone has eaten well and has clean clothes. Soon everyone will go to sleep in neat, orderly rooms. I have helped with all that. It is partly because of my work that the house of Han is at peace."

She looked down at Jade and stroked her hair. "It is a very satisfying feeling, Jade. And someday you too will feel it. This is what I wish for you."

In the touch of the gentle hand on her hair, Jade felt forgiveness. But part of her was still uneasy. She turned her head and looked up into her mother's face.

"Mother," she whispered.

"Yes?"

"This feeling that you speak of. Is it enough for your happiness?"

Jade thought her mother looked sad for just a moment, but then her face was smooth again. "Yes, Jade," she answered. "I have learned to make it enough."

Different Rules

There was an eerie tension among the adults the next day. Jade noticed it at once. Her mother was stern and tightlipped at the morning meal, the aunts quiet and fearful. At first Jade thought it was because of her escape, but gradually she realized that it must be something more.

Her father and uncles did not speak as Jade tiptoed among them serving their food, but that in itself was not unusual. It was considered bad manners to speak while eating. It was the heaviness of their silence that worried Jade, and the way her uncles kept stealing furtive glances at her father.

The news of her escape could not have been the cause. It would have been equally poor manners for any of the men to show disapproval, for her punishment had been dealt with by her mother. It was not their business to concern themselves about her misdeed.

Later that morning she met Tiger in the garden. Jade had so many questions for him that she hardly knew where to begin. The atmosphere that lay over the house made her whisper.

"Brother, yesterday I saw some strange men being taken to the palace. They had broken the law, someone said." Jade swallowed nervously. "Who are these men? What did they do? Does it have something to do with our father?"

Tiger Heart looked almost terrified. "Sister, these are truly not matters of your concern. You must not ask such questions."

Jade was astonished. "Brother, I know it was wrong of me to leave the Inner Court. But surely you can tell me something about what I saw."

Tiger looked around the garden as if someone might be listening. "Our father has told me a little of these matters, but I do not really understand. I know only that those men come from a land far, far from here. Their ship crashed into Cheju Island during a storm several months ago, and now they have been brought here for the King to decide their fate.

"The sailors say that they were headed for Japan, but who knows if they are telling the truth. Perhaps they intended to come here all along. No such strangers have been allowed in Korea for nearly a hundred years. There are many in our King's court who are angry. They believe all such strangers should be killed.

"But our father thinks it would be far better not to show fear of these men. He tells me that they might bring new ideas to Korea, and that perhaps we could learn from them.

"Our father does not want such men to be killed. The King's court is in great disagreement now. No one knows what the King will decide."

Jade shook her head in worry and bemusement. She was about to ask more questions when Tiger changed the subject abruptly. He informed her that the servant who had been driving the cart had been dismissed by their father.

Jade looked aghast. "But Brother! It's not fair! It wasn't his fault—he didn't even know I was there!"

Tiger looked at her sternly. In some way Jade felt that he had understood why she had attempted her escape, and he had not said one word against it—until now. "Jade, it is not your place to question the actions of our father."

Jade's heart ached when she thought of how her rash plan had cost a man his job. She remembered how he had tried his best to cover her with the cloth, and realized that he must have felt doomed from the moment he laid eyes on her. She sighed, but for the moment her thoughts turned to something else.

"Brother, the next time you go to the marketplace, I need you to do me a favor. Please give my share of sweets to the child of Chang the cabbage seller. His stall is the third on the right, and the child is the age of our brother, Mountain Wind."

Tiger was exasperated. "Sister, don't you think this adventure should be behind you now?"

"It is, Brother. But I made a promise, and I must keep it."

Tiger relented. "Just this once. If I start handing out sweets, every urchin in town will be begging from me."

It was not a compromise that satisfied Jade; she had planned to ask Tiger to give the child her share of sweets on a regular basis. She had had time to reflect on their encounter, and recalled how the child had made three sweets sound like a king's treasure. . . . Tiger brought her at least a dozen sweets at a time. The memory of the child's lively eyes and friendly manner had become one of the few highlights of her forlorn adventure. But Jade had still more questions.

"Brother, when I was out on the road, I saw many women and girls. Are they always there? How is it that they leave their Inner Courts?"

Tiger looked puzzled, then uncomfortable. "Their families are different," he mumbled.

"Different? What do you mean? Don't they care that strange men see them all the time?"

Tiger considered for a moment. "You know our servants. They live with us, and earn money, and once a year they go home to visit their own families."

Jade sat still, trying hard to understand. She knew that the servants left once a year, at different times, depending on when they could most easily be spared from their work. The gardener left for several days during the winter. The cook left in the spring, during a stretch of time when there were no feast days. But Jade had never thought to wonder where they went when they left.

"What does that have to do with the girls out there on the road?"

"Jade, not everyone lives as we do. Those women and girls, their families are poor—even poorer than our servants. Everyone in their families has to work—"

"Everyone? Even the girls?"

"They live in a different way—they don't have the same rules—" Tiger stumbled over his words as he tried to explain.

Jade thought some more about the people she had seen. She had not thought much of it then, but now she could remember their rough clothing, unkempt hair, and bare feet. And in her mind she had an image of Willow in her silk robes, carried aloft in her sedan chair, while behind her the little Chang child scrabbled for sweets in the dirt.

A Humble Request

Jade paused before the door of the finest room in the men's quarters. But she hesitated for only a moment, for she knew if she stood there any longer, she would lose her courage. She cleared her throat and called quietly.

"*Abu-ji?*" Hoping from the outset to communicate her respect, Jade used the most formal word for "father," not the more affectionate *Ah-pa.*

The paper door slid open. Jade's father, head of the Han household, stood in the doorway. Although, as always, his face showed no emotion, Jade thought that he looked very tired.

"Good evening, Daughter. Have you eaten well?" He returned her greeting with equal formality.

In truth, Jade did not know her father very well. It was the custom in noble families for the father to attend to his work and the family's financial matters, the mother to deal with the children and the household affairs. In recent years Tiger had seen a great deal of their father, as he was being groomed to become head of the household himself one day. But the other children—Jade and little Mountain Wind, her younger brother—were entrusted to their mother's care. On feast days and at other family celebrations their father might honor them with a small gift or perhaps tell them stories of the wonders of the King's court. Otherwise, the children left him to his business, and he left them to theirs.

So it was with great trepidation that Jade had approached him that evening. She knew that what she had to say would not please him, and it would serve to remind him of her recent dishonorable behavior. But after two days and as many sleepless nights, she knew she no longer had a choice in the matter. She had to speak.

"Yes, thank you, Father."

"Please come in." Jade stepped into the room, and her father closed the door behind her.

It was a beautiful room. The walls were hung with precious scrolls by the most famous of the country's writers and artists. A rare tiger-skin rug covered part of the floor. And in a specially made niche stood the wondrous ivory ball.

She looked at it now, as she sat on the floor before her father's low table, and its familiar puzzle comforted her. Her own ivory ball was in her pocket, as a reminder of her father's rarely shown affection. She took a deep breath and bowed her head.

"Honorable Father, I am sorry to disturb you this evening. But I have something to ask of you."

Her father did not reply. He merely gestured with his hand for her to continue.

"When I behaved so dishonorably the other day"—Jade kept her head bowed and did not look at her father—"I did so with no one else's knowledge. Servant Cho did not know that I was in the cart when he left the house."

Jade paused. She had rehearsed her words many times in her head, but now she was coming to the most delicate part of her speech.

Her father waited.

"I do not question my honorable father's wisdom in his actions. But I humbly request that he allow Servant Cho back into our household. With your permission, I would like to explain why."

Jade's father was silent. Unsure of what to do, Jade finally decided to take his silence as permission.

"When Servant Cho saw me at the marketplace, he showed great concern for our family's honor. He ran into the

marketplace at once and bought cloth to cover me. He made sure that I was hidden from the eyes of strange men all the way home. In every way he acted as a loyal servant to our family. I do not wish him to be punished for my mistake."

That was all. It had taken Jade so long to find the words, and only a few seconds to say them. She could do nothing now but wait.

After what felt like an eternity, her father spoke.

"Right behavior is indeed important, Daughter. It is one of the Five Virtues. Your brother has been learning much about them. Right behavior, good form, wisdom, faith, and love. They are small words, but they hold all that is good about men."

He rose to his feet. He fetched the ivory ball from its place on the shelf, seated himself again, and began turning the ball slowly in his hands as if studying it closely. But Jade could see that his thoughts were elsewhere.

He started to speak, then hesitated. At last he seemed to make up his mind about something, and spoke. "You saw the men on the road the other day? The strangers?"

"Yes, Father."

"Those men, they do not believe in the Five Virtues. They speak of other laws, other kings, other lands. There are those who are angry that they should dare challenge Confucius' teachings, but our King wishes to understand these men. At his request I have spoken with them myself on many occasions. And though we have many differences, there are things about their laws that are in harmony with ours."

Jade's father looked up from the ball, but his eyes were focused on some place or something not in the room. He continued to speak quietly. "I believe we have much to learn from each other. It is time for our people to look beyond our borders. We have kept to ourselves for too long."

It was an uncharacteristically long speech—indeed, the greatest number of words Jade had ever heard her father speak. Suddenly he seemed to realize that she was still there; he glanced at her, replaced the ball carefully in its niche, and walked to the door. It was the signal that their meeting was at an end. Jade stood and bowed to her father.

Her father nodded to her. As she prepared to leave, he said one more thing.

"I do not forget, Daughter, that right behavior is only one of the Five Virtues."

And the door closed behind her.

Royal Decision

It seemed to Jade that she would never find the chance to speak to Tiger alone. It had been several days since her escape and then her conversation with her father—days during which her father had spent most of his time at the palace. Some days he had not returned home at all.

Yesterday had been a momentous day. The King had heard from all those at the court who wished to express an opinion on the fate of the prisoners. Jade was sure that her father would have been among those to speak, and she felt almost frantic with desire to learn what he had said.

For the first time in his life Tiger had accompanied his father to the King's court. He had been among the crowd inside the palace walls; he had heard everything that had been said. But since his return in the evening Jade had not seen him except while she served the men and boys their meals.

Late during the following afternoon Jade loitered about the men's quarters, hoping to catch Tiger coming or going. Her efforts were at last rewarded; when Tiger came out of his room, Jade stepped forward from a corner.

"Brother! Please, can we talk for a moment?"

Tiger did not look surprised to see her. "I was just coming to find you," he said. "Come, let's go for a walk in the garden."

They walked in silence until they reached the little bridge and stood there together as dusk strengthened the shadows. Then Tiger Heart began to speak.

"I am to tell you what I saw and heard yesterday, Jade," he said slowly. "It is our father who requests that I do so."

Jade's surprise was so great that her body stiffened; her brother glanced at her quickly. "Our father has told me that, as you already know, these events are not the affairs of women. But he also knows what you saw that day, and he believes that unanswered curiosity can build a road to danger. I will tell you what I know."

Jade nodded solemnly, grateful beyond words for her father's understanding.

"First, you must picture this: The King sits on a throne at the head of a wide set of stairs. His guards and ministers stand or sit on either side of him. Anyone who wishes to address him comes to the foot of the stairs and speaks to him from there. The rest of the room is full of other people—junior ministers, scholars, royal retainers, servants. I was lucky; as we had arrived early, I had a position near the stairs. Otherwise, it is very difficult to hear.

"Many people spoke. I cannot remember everything that they said, but it was easy enough to see that most of the court wanted the prisoners beheaded. Adviser after adviser spoke to the King about their insolence and treachery—that they say there are kingdoms far greater than our own, greater than China, even, and that our Five Virtues are not enough. They speak of ten laws, written in a little book they all carry. The advisers believe they are enemies of the worst kind.

"All day long such men spoke. Believe me, Jade—being able to leave our household is not always a wonderful thing. There were times yesterday when I thought I would die of boredom." Tiger turned to her with a wry grin.

But Jade was too anxious to respond to his gentle teasing. "Please, Brother, go on."

Tiger grew sober again. "At last our father took his turn. He spoke for only a few minutes. And yet, what he said . . ." Tiger paused, deep in thought. "Perhaps it is only because he is my father, but I do not think so. His words had great power; you could see it in the faces of all who were there.

"He began by speaking of the men. They were not a great

army—just a few sailors. If they truly wanted to topple the King, would they have come here in such small numbers?

"Then he spoke of the harm that grows from ignorance. We know very little about these men and their ways, he said. Supposing they are friends, it would be a terrible injustice to execute them. And if they are not, it is always best to know as much as possible about one's enemies. It would serve the King well to let these men live so that more could be learned from them.

"Our father told the King that, as it now stands, we do not know enough. He finished by saying that the path to wisdom lies not in certainty, but in trying to understand."

Tiger's voice had grown in strength as he spoke of his father's words. Jade had a sudden inkling of the future. One day, she realized, it would be Tiger who spoke before the King.

Tiger continued, "After all had spoken, the King withdrew to his chambers, to consult with his Council. Our father, as you know, is a member of the Council. It took a long time, but they finally reached a decision.

"The men are not to be beheaded, nor will they be allowed to return to their homes. They must remain here in Korea and swear allegiance to the King. If they will do so, they will be given positions in the army and may live here freely.

"Our father's desire was that these men be allowed to come and go as they please, between our country and theirs. He believes it is time for us to know more of the world. The King did not agree, but neither did he heed those who were calling for the men to be killed. His decision, Father says, walks in the middle of the path."

Tiger Heart seemed to feel there had been enough serious talk. He finished by saying that the prisoners had been brought in to hear of the King's decision. "I know they are men, Jade, but from all the hair on their faces, you might think they were a kind of man-bear!"

Jade smiled gratefully at him. For once she did not have to imagine something she had never seen.

A Mountain of Stitches

Jade's mother inspected the small scrap of fabric carefully. On it Jade had stitched a many-petaled yellow-and-white chrysanthemum. It was the work of many painstaking days. Jade held her breath as her mother turned the scrap over. No knots or loose threads showed. The back and front were mirror-perfect.

Jade's mother did not smile, but her eyes twinkled.

"Yes, Jade. You are ready. You may begin your first panel."

Jade let out her breath. An embroidered screen of many panels was one of the things a well-bred girl made for her wedding dowry. Only a few months ago it had seemed to Jade that her own wedding day was still far away. But Willow's marriage had changed all that. Jade tried not to think about the day that she would leave her home. She concentrated instead on the knowledge that being allowed to begin her screen was a sign that her embroidery skills had reached a high level indeed.

Jade began to plan her first panel. Once—it seemed long since—she had thought of embroidering the cranes she had seen flying over the house, but all memory of them had vanished in the face of her first glimpse of the mountains that day on the road. It was the mountains she would depict on her panel.

Jade knew what they should look like. They would be a misty blue-gray color, with white on top. There would be bright green rice fields at the bottom. She chose her colors carefully.

Somehow the mountains had gotten tangled up in her mind with the strangers, with Willow's refusal to see her, and with Servant Cho's misfortune. They remained a background of steady reassurance in a scene of confusion and pain.

The time she spent planning her panel took her mind off the fact that Servant Cho had not been rehired. At first Jade had hoped that the events at the court had been keeping her father too busy to attend to the matter. But the days went by, and Servant Cho did not reappear. She had failed.

Her mother brought out the precious bolt of blue silk, dark as the night sky. It had been saved especially for this purpose. She measured and cut the proper length. "Have you chosen your subject?"

"Yes, Mother," Jade answered. She hesitated only a moment. "I wish to show the noble mountains that guard Seoul, where the graves of our ancestors lie."

Jade's mother looked at her sharply. But her voice was gentle as she said, "That is not the usual subject for a panel, Jade. Have you considered, perhaps, a peony blossom or a water lily? Your flowers are very fine. They would make an excellent panel."

Jade had been prepared for this response. She spoke respectfully but firmly. "If it would not displease my honorable mother, I would like to show the mountains. I know that it is not usually done, but it is my wish to try."

Jade's mother sighed almost inaudibly. "All right, if it is your wish. But I think you will soon find that they do not make a good subject."

Jade took the length of blue silk, vowing silently to prove her mother wrong.

It took only a few attempts for Jade to learn that her mother knew far more about embroidery than she did. The texture of the thread on the silk *was* somehow wrong for mountains. The tiny, fine stitches that melded together so smoothly to show a flower petal or a fish's shiny scales would not make the greatness and solidity of mountains.

Jade tried different stitches. She changed colors often. She picked out as many stitches as she put in. She worked so long and hard that her fingers were raw from the needle and her back and shoulders ached from bending over.

Her mother tried to tease her gently. "You need not work so hard on the panel, Jade. You have plenty of time before the matchmaker comes!"

Jade heard the worry in her mother's voice and smiled half-heartedly in response. But when her mother turned away, Jade sewed all the more stubbornly.

Her stitches were only part of the problem. Each day she feared that her memory of the mountains was fading, little by little. From the special spot in the garden, she would stare at what little she could discern of the peaks, then close her eyes, trying to remember what she had seen from the seat of the cart that day. Jade had first thought she would never forget how the mountains looked in their entirety. But her failure to embroider them as she wished combined with the passing of time to make her feel as if those same heavy clouds were slowly closing in over the picture in her mind.

Brushes and Scrolls

Schoolmaster was ill. He had woken one morning with a bad spirit of sickness in his head and had been in bed for several days now. Jade's mother sent special soups and tonics every morning and evening, and he would soon be well. But for the time being the boys had no classes.

Tiger Heart alone among the boys still went to the Hall of Learning each day to study on his own. In a few years he would take examinations at the King's court. He would have to do well to become a royal scholar like his father.

One afternoon Jade put down her embroidery in despair. She stretched her aching back and shoulders and took a walk around the Inner Court. The door to the Hall of Learning was open, and she saw Tiger bent over his books. She stepped inside quietly. The Hall was forbidden to girls only during the boys' lessons, but Jade had not been in the room since the day of her prank with Willow.

She liked the Hall of Learning. Many beautiful scrolls hung on the walls, with elegant calligraphy for the boys to copy. Jade could not read, but she knew by heart some of the poems written on the scrolls. Rolls of fine rice paper and porcelain jars of ink were arranged on the shelves, next to the rabbit-hair brushes. It felt like a place of wisdom.

It was winter, and while there was not much snow outside, the air was still frosty. But the stone floors of each room in the house were always warm and cozy because of the long pipes underneath that reached all the way to the kitchen stove. Jade crossed the room to the low table where Tiger was reading and sat down next to him, grateful for the warmth that rose through the floor's waxed-paper tiles.

"What are you reading?" Jade asked.

"It's a scroll about Tan-gun," Tiger answered. The famous story about the founder of their nation was familiar to all Korean children, but Tiger had to know every word perfectly for his examinations.

Jade bent over his shoulder and let out a gasp of surprise. In the middle of the scroll was a picture of two mountains. Between them a graceful swash of ink made a river. A few tiny, deft brushstrokes indicated a man near the river.

"That's Tan-gun." Tiger pointed. "He will escape from his enemy by crossing the river."

Jade hardly heard him. The mountains in the picture looked almost as they had when she had seen them from the road. Here was the magnificence and mystery and reassurance she had felt. Here was the way to keep the picture forever, not with thread on silk but with ink on paper.

"Brother, can I try that?"

Tiger looked surprised. "What, reading it? You don't know how to read."

"No, no, not reading it. I want to try to paint—to make a picture like that."

Tiger wrinkled his brow. "I don't know . . . Schoolmaster might not like it."

"He won't know; he's still sick in bed. Just a small bit of paper, Brother, please!"

Tiger shrugged. He unrolled a few inches of rice paper and tore the piece off carefully. Jade fetched a brush and ink from the shelves and eagerly began to paint a line across the paper.

Tiger watched her for a moment, then took the brush from her impatiently. "You're using too much ink," he said. "Here—" He wiped the brush gently and gave it back to her. "And don't press so hard. Master says it should be like a butterfly's wing."

Jade tried again. Tiger nodded. "That's much better." He watched in silence for a few minutes longer.

"By the way," he said, his eyes still on the paper, "I thought you would like to know. Servant Cho has a new job with the Kim family. It was our father who recommended him for the position." He looked up to return her grin of delight, then went back to his studies.

As Tiger bent over the scroll again, Jade worked to try to copy the picture of the mountains. Her lines were heavy and clumsy, unlike the delicate strokes on the scroll, and she tried again and again until at last she drew a single line that satisfied her. Tiger glanced up for a moment and nodded at her work. "It's not bad for your first try."

Jade was thrilled with his praise. That afternoon she worked until the strip of paper was full. She could hardly believe how much time had passed when the dinner gong sounded. There was joy in the gentle strokes of the brush—joy at learning of Cho's good fortune, relief that her mistake had not been his permanent doom.

And every afternoon until the Master was well, she slipped into the Hall of Learning to paint again.

Yut Sticks

Jade's attempts at painting continued. She begged scraps of paper from Tiger. He even smuggled a brush and a jar of ink out of the Hall of Learning for her. As he gave them to her, he said, "There you are. But why would a girl want to paint?" Jade could not have told him why—only that she *had* to paint, to put the pictures in her head onto paper, where she could see them with her eyes.

While she did not wish to deceive her mother, Jade painted only when she was sure to be alone—in her room, or in a quiet corner of the garden when her mother was busy. She knew what her mother would say if she should learn of Jade's new interest. Painting was a noble art, reserved for men.

As a consequence of her secret painting, Jade had abandoned her attempt to embroider the mountains. To her mother's satisfaction, the swordlike leaves and rich purple blooms of iris plants were slowly taking shape on Jade's first panel.

Pleased as she was with her embroidery, Jade was still dissatisfied with her painting. She could not show anyone her attempts, nor ask questions about how to improve her work. She could only experiment, with different brushes and strokes, wet paper, dry paper, rubbing, shading, blotting—and starting all over again. Jade was sure that no other painter used as much ink as she did.

Beyond her efforts to discover good technique, Jade felt desperate to see the mountains again—not just once, but many times. The pictures that most pleased her were of things she had looked at as she was painting: the bridge over the pond, a willow tree, her little ivory ball. But whenever she tried to paint the mountains from memory, there always seemed to be something missing.

As she frowned over her most recent picture of the mountains, she felt she had no way of knowing whether she was putting a true picture on the paper. *I must see beyond the wall again*, she thought. *There must be a way*.

Jade did not consider another attempt at escape. The

first had been disastrous. Alone, she walked in the garden; overhead, she could see blue sky and wild birds flying. *If only I could fly*, she thought.

If only I could fly.

The following month, it was time for the New Year celebration. This was great fun for all the family. The children bowed in front of their elders and received gifts of money. Jade was delighted. Although she had bowed every year since she had been a small child, she had never used the money for anything but sweets. Now she had enough to give Tiger to buy paper and ink the next time he went to the market.

The festivities lasted for several days. Everyone ate wonderful food and played games. Jade's favorite game was *yut*. It was a board game popular with both adults and children. *Yut* was played with long smooth sticks, each with a rounded side and a flat side. A player tossed the *yut* sticks into the air; the flat sides that landed faceup indicated the number of spaces a token could be moved.

On the last day of the New Year celebration, Jade grew tired of *yut* and stood by watching some of her cousins play. One of the youngest, little Dragon Fire, had taken an extra set of *yut* sticks and tokens. He was playing his own game with them—balancing one stick across another, putting a token at the end, and then pounding the other end with his hand. As the token flipped into the air, Dragon squealed with delight and tried to catch it.

Jade watched him, first idly, then with growing interest. When Dragon balanced the token just right and hit the other end just so, the token flipped high into the air.

Another plan began to grow in Jade's mind.

Jade watched for her chance. Soon the spring season's repairs began. As always, winter snow and winds had done some damage to the house, and masons and carpenters arrived to make their repairs. It was a boring time for the girls of the Han household, for while the workers were busy in the Inner Court, the girls had to stay behind closed doors.

But the repairs were finished quickly, and soon the girls were free to roam the Inner Court again. Jade wandered about noticing the work that had been done here and there. There was debris in some corners that had not yet been cleared away by the servants. And in one pile Jade found just what she needed: a long wooden board.

Jade wheedled one of the servants into carrying the board to the garden for her. She got Tiger to bring her one of the tightly rolled sheaves of rice-straw that were kept in the stables to feed the oxen. After a few experiments, her invention was ready.

Beyond the Walls

Jade needed one more thing—a partner. She was slowly growing accustomed to Willow's absence, but there were times like now when she sorely missed her old friend. Jade had to think carefully about whom to choose. She needed someone old enough to follow instructions well, but younger than herself so he or she could be coaxed into doing what needed to be done.

Only two of her cousins were suitable—a shy girl named Moon Lily and a boy named Bear Courage. She decided to try Lily first. Lily was younger and shorter than Jade, but a little plumper. Jade approached her with great friendliness.

"Lily, would you like to play a new game with me? It's in the garden."

Lily was cautious. "What kind of new game, Cousin?"

"It doesn't have a name. But I'm sure you'll like it." In the end Lily agreed and followed Jade to the garden.

In the middle of a clearing was a simple contraption. The sheaf of straw lay on the ground with the wooden board across it.

Lily stared at it curiously. "What is it, Cousin?"

"I'll show you. It's a jumping game." Jade stepped onto one end of the board. "Now, I want you to stand at the other end, jump off the ground as high as you can, and land on the board."

Lily shrugged and did as she was told. The results were unexpected.

When Lily hit her end of the board, Jade did indeed pop up off the other end. But she lost all control in the air and landed in a heap on the ground, one shoe flying off and her skirts in a tangle.

Lily ran shrieking to her cousin's side, her eyes wide with fear. Jade sat up, rubbing her ankle. "I'm all right," she said impatiently. She limped over and put on her shoe. "It worked fine—we just need to practice more." But Lily backed away in alarm, shaking her head. No amount of coaxing or pleading could persuade her to try again.

Now Jade had to try her plan with Bear Courage. He too

was younger, but not as easily led as Lily. He was busy playing ball and did not want to try her new game.

Jade tried everything she could think of. She pleaded, cajoled, even threatened him. Nothing worked. At last in desperation, she thought of bribery.

"Bear, Tiger goes to the market tomorrow. He always brings me sweets. If you come with me now, I'll give you my share of the sweets."

For the first time, Bear looked interested. "*All* of your share?"

Jade nodded. "All of it."

Bear considered. "Not enough. I want something more for playing a girl's game."

Jade thought hard. She ran to her room and opened the lacquer chest where she kept her things. The silk purse that held her ivory ball was carefully stored in its usual place in one corner.

With the ivory ball clutched in her fist, Jade ran back across the Inner Court. Halfway to the garden she slowed to a walk and finally halted. She opened her hand and studied the little ball, rolling it around in her palm.

How many memories it held! Jade recalled her delight when her father had given it to her, and the many times she had played hide-and-find with Willow in the garden. The little ball had been with her during her escape. And many times in recent months Jade had painted it, trying to capture perfectly its carvings and curves.

She closed her hand tightly over it again. *If my plan works*, she told herself fiercely, *I will see things even more wondrous than my ball.*

"Look, Bear." She opened her hand. Bear's eyes widened. He reached for the ball. Jade pulled her hand back. "You have to play whenever I want," she demanded.

Bear agreed, and with one last pang in her heart, Jade handed over the ball.

Bear was a much better partner than Lily. He thought it great fun to send Jade flying from her end of the board and didn't worry when she fell down. But Jade's invention was not working as she had hoped. She did not get high enough to see over the wall.

At last Bear grew tired of jumping on his end and demanded that Jade jump to send him flying. Jade did not want to give up her chance to see over the wall. She thought for a moment.

"Bear, I want to try something different. This time, when you jump and send me up in the air, I'm not going to land on the ground. I'm going to land on the board again. So when I land on the board, you'll go flying."

Bear agreed eagerly. After a few attempts, they found that it worked; not only that, but Bear's turn in the air was higher than Jade's.

"Let's keep going!" shouted Bear. "We don't have to stop after one jump each—let's see how many we can do!"

Bear's idea was a good one. By the end of the afternoon,

they were doing five or six jumps each. It took great concentration and timing, for the jumper had to jump at the exact moment that the "flyer" landed. But when they did it right, each flight was higher than the one before. Jade was having so much fun that she almost forgot to look over the wall.

The predinner gong sounded; it was time for Jade to go help prepare the evening meal. "One more time!" yelled Bear.

Jade stood on her end and waited for Bear's jump. Up into air she went, then down, then up again, higher than before. This time she remembered to look over the wall.

She saw the streets outside the Outer Wall. She saw people. Each time she jumped, she saw something else— the rice fields, a stray dog, a farmer and his donkey. And on her last jump, she saw the mountains.

She saw them in the dusk, purple-blue this time against the bluer sky. As she flew through the air, she glimpsed them only for an instant, but it was long enough for her to make a picture in her mind—a picture that she would paint as truly as she was able.

Jade ran to the kitchens in a daze of delight. Jumping on the seesaw had felt almost like flying. She thought about the flashes of life she had seen outside the wall—above all, her glimpse of the mountains. Jade hoped with all her heart that with the seesaw's help she would be able to see the mountains as Tiger had described them so many times.

She wanted to see their colors change in the fall, and the

snow frosting them like rice powder in the winter. She wanted to paint them rising like ghosts from the fog and blazing with glory in a sunrise. And one day, perhaps very soon, she would see for herself the long snake of people climbing the mountain on an ancestral feast day.

In the flush of her success Jade even thought wildly that she might one day be able to glimpse over the mountains themselves, to whatever lay beyond them.

It's not enough, she thought. *But I will learn to make it enough.*

And she felt as though she had wings on her feet as she hurried with the bowl of rice so the men would not have to wait for their evening meal.

AUTHOR'S NOTE

Beginning in the sixteenth century, Korea followed a policy of isolationism. For nearly three hundred years contact was maintained only with China and, to a lesser and more hostile extent, with Japan; Korea acquired the nickname "The Hermit Kingdom."

In the 1600s, when this story is set, Dutch explorers reached Korea for the first time. Attempting to sail from China to Japan, the *Sperwer* (Sparrow), with thirty-two sailors aboard, lost its way during a storm and ran aground at Cheju Island off the south coast of Korea. The sailors were detained in Korea from 1653 to 1666, when a handful of them escaped to Japan.

Among them was Hendrik Hamel, who kept a journal about his experiences. For the purposes of the story, I have taken a slight liberty with the actual dates of certain events recorded by Hamel. The Dutch sailors were taken to Seoul in 1654 and lived under house arrest for nearly two years; it was not until 1656 that a final decision was made to allow them to live.

Communication with the sailors initially took place via the interpretive efforts of a Dutch sailor who had been shipwrecked some twenty-five years earlier. Jan Weltevree had also been forbidden to leave the country, and had settled into life there as an adviser to the military, introducing the cannon to Korea.

Korea continued to repel foreign visitors until 1882, when its first treaties with the Western world were signed. It would have been not Tiger Heart himself but his descendants who eventually brought about this change.

The lives of aristocratic women and girls throughout the Choson period in Korea (1300–1880) were severely circumscribed. A girl lived in her family home until she married, after which she moved to her husband's home. She might be permitted to visit her parents' home for special celebrations, and she usually attended their funerals; however, after marriage a woman was considered a member of her husband's family, not the family in which she had grown up. This is why there is no mention of Jade's maternal grandparents in this story.

Sometime during the Choson period, a policy was instituted requiring all men to be indoors after dark. Women were then allowed to walk the streets without fear of being seen by strange men. The women would throw long coats over their heads in case there were men about who disobeyed the law. Many visitors to Korea in the nineteenth century remarked on this custom; however, Hamel does not mention it in his journal, so perhaps the policy was not in place at that time. In telling Jade's story, I tried to imagine a life with as little access to the outside world as possible, so the nighttime excursions were not included.

The artists and writers in Jade Blossom's time were all

men. Girls received no formal education, practically their only artistic outlet was embroidery. But while she would not have been able to read or write, a girl did not need a formal education to become a painter. It would have been a great struggle for her, but in every place and age there have been people possessed of such courage.

There is a famous image in Korean art of the mountains as seen in the distance from behind the walls of the city. I like to think that at least a few of the anonymous renditions of this image were painted by women—women who, as girls like Jade, had a great yearning to see beyond the wall.

The "standing and jumping" seesaw has been used in Korea for hundreds of years; indeed, the "sitting-down" seesaw was unknown there until the years of American influence after World War II. As indicated by Bear's enthusiasm, the seesaw was popular among both young girls and boys, although by the time boys reached their teenage years, they disdained it as a girls' game. In a further refinement, a third person squats in the center of the board to keep it from slipping off the fulcrum.

When I was growing up, my mother made a Korean seesaw in the backyard of our Chicago suburban home. It took a lot of practice, but once my brother and I learned how to use it, we had great fun sending each other flying into the air. And I have a Korean seesaw in my backyard for my own children.

Jade Blossom's seesaw is still used in Korea today.

BIBLIOGRAPHY

Carpenter, Francis. *Tales of a Korean Grandmother*. Rutland, Vt.: Tuttle, 1973.

Clark, Donald N. *Christianity in Modern Korea*. Lanham, Md.: University Press of America; New York: Asia Society, 1986.

Cumings, Bruce. *Korea's Place in the Sun: A Modern History*. New York: Norton, 1997.

Eckhert, Carter, et al. *Korea Old and New: A History*. Seoul, Korea: Korea Institute, Harvard University, 1990.

Hamel, Hendrik. *Hamel's Journal and a Description of the Kingdom of Korea, 1653–1666*. Translated by Br. Jean-Paul Buys of Taize. Seoul, Korea: Royal Asiatic Society, 1994.

Hunter, Ruth, and Debra Fritsch. *A Part of the Ribbon*. Hartford, Conn.: Turtle Press, 1997.

Hyegyonggung, Hong Ssi. *Memoirs of Lady Hyegyong*. Translated and edited by JaHyun Kim Haboush. Berkeley: University of California Press, 1996.

Keith, Elizabeth, and Elspet Keith Robertson Scott. *Old Korea: The Land of the Morning Calm*. New York: Philosophical Library, 1947.

Wright, Chris. *Korea: Its History and Culture*. Seoul, Korea: Korean Overseas Information Service, 1994.

Yoo, Yushin. *Korea the Beautiful: Treasures of the Hermit Kingdom*. Los Angeles: Golden Pond Press, 1987.

Have you read these other Yearling favorites?

0-440-41231-5

0-440-41641-8

0-440-40917-9

0-440-41648-5

0-440-41651-5

0-440-41496-2

0-440-41538-1

Available now from Yearling Books